This book belongs to:

....

....

....

CONTENTS

Published by

X-30, Okhla Industrial Area Phase-II,New Delhi-110020, INDIA
Tel.: 011-41611861, 40712200, Fax: 011-41611866
E-mail: sales@dpb.in

Edited by Pratibha Kasturia
Illustrated by Pankaj

Printed by: Best Photo Offset Printers, A-81, D.D.A. Sheds,
Okhla Industrial Area, Phase-II, New Delhi-110020

www.juniordiamond.com

BULL'S MILK

Once upon a time, Emperor Akbar fell sick. A doctor was called. The doctor examined the king and gave him some medicines, saying, "This medicine will cure you immediately. But you must take it with bull's milk only."

The doctor had old enmity with Birbal. So, he played this trick to put Birbal in difficulty. King Akbar called Birbal and ordered him, "I want bull's milk. Go and bring it at any cost."

Birbal went home. His daughter noticed that her father was looking very sad and disturbed. She asked him the reason for his anxiety. Birbal told her everything. He was very much worried.

Like Birbal, his daughter was also very intelligent. Both of them thought of a plan. Birbal sent his daughter to wash clothes at the royal pond at midnight. She went there and started washing clothes. Akbar's sleep was disturbed. He sent the guards to bring the girl to him.

"Why are you washing clothes at such odd an hour?" The king asked. "O King! My father has given birth to a baby today. He is confined to bed. I didn't get time during the day. So, I am washing clothes now," replied the girl.

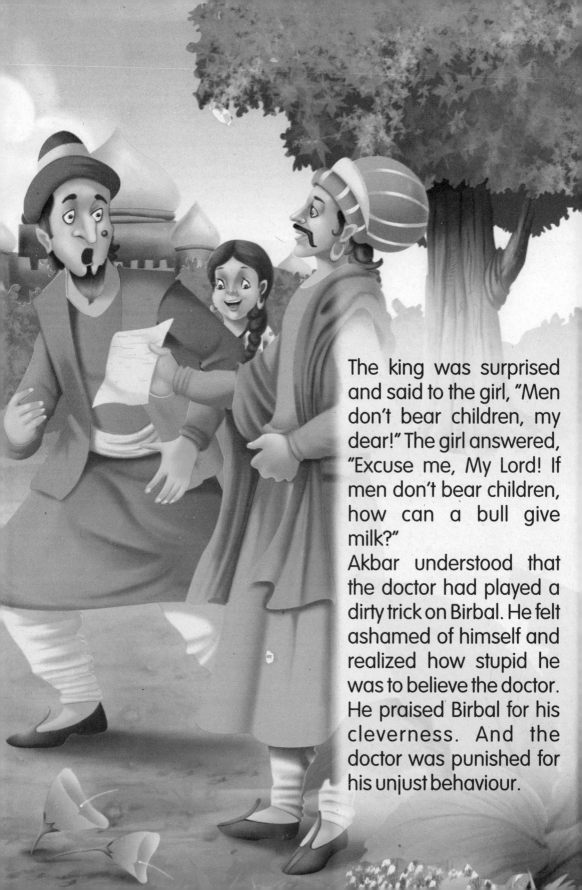

The king was surprised and said to the girl, "Men don't bear children, my dear!" The girl answered, "Excuse me, My Lord! If men don't bear children, how can a bull give milk?"

Akbar understood that the doctor had played a dirty trick on Birbal. He felt ashamed of himself and realized how stupid he was to believe the doctor. He praised Birbal for his cleverness. And the doctor was punished for his unjust behaviour.

BIRBAL'S JOURNEY TO HEAVEN

Once upon a time, some jealous courtiers in Akbar's court, hatched a conspiracy to get Birbal killed. They persuaded the king's barber to execute their plan. They offered him some gold coins as a reward.

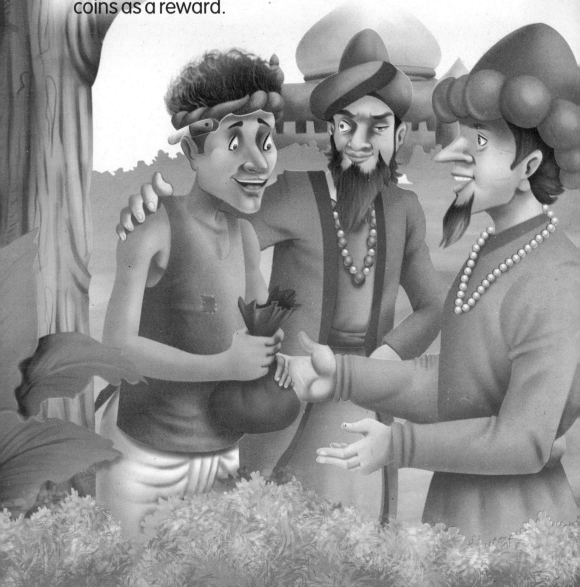

The next morning, while attending to the king, the barber said, "Your Highness! You should send a wise man like Birbal to heaven to inquire about your ancestors' well-being." The king liked the idea.

In the court, the king disclosed his plan to send Birbal to heaven. As suggested by the barber, he announced, "Birbal will sit on a pyre which will be set on fire. With its smoke, Birbal will reach heaven."

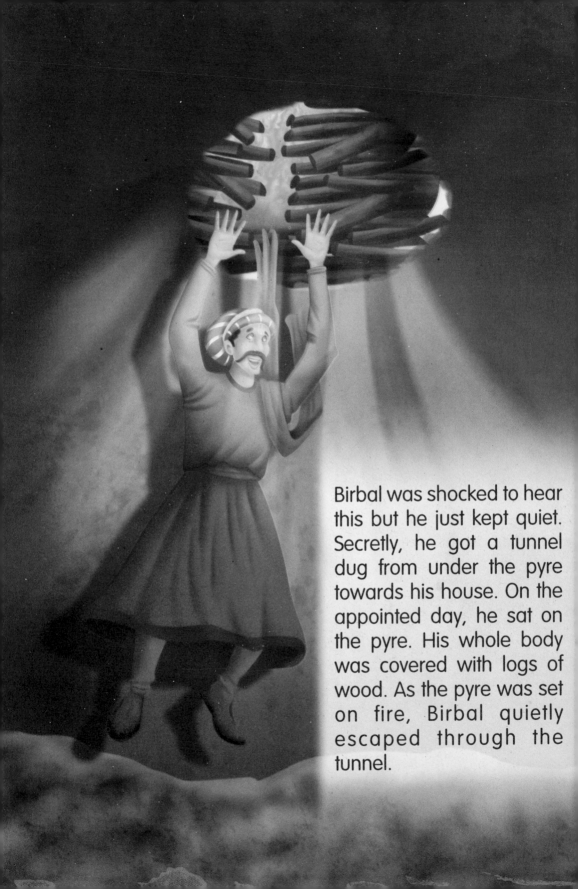

Birbal was shocked to hear this but he just kept quiet. Secretly, he got a tunnel dug from under the pyre towards his house. On the appointed day, he sat on the pyre. His whole body was covered with logs of wood. As the pyre was set on fire, Birbal quietly escaped through the tunnel.

He reached his home safely by using that tunnel. No one knew that Birbal was at home. He changed his appearance and came out of his house. He went around the town in disguise to find out the people who were involved in the conspiracy to kill him. He found out all the names after the hard work of a few days.

After a few days, Birbal appeared in the King's court. He said, "Your Highness! Your ancestors are fine there. However, they are very worried about their long-grown beards. They have asked me to send your barber and the courtiers to heaven immediately."

The king agreed and ordered for the arrangements to be made. The barber and the courtiers were shocked. They had no other way but to obey Akbar's order. However, they realized that it was not easy to befool clever Birbal.

THE MERCHANT AND THE GOLD COIN

Once a merchant came to Birbal to get justice. He said, "Sir, long ago, a friend of mine had borrowed one thousand Rupees from me. But now, he is refusing to pay back my money." Birbal assured him that justice shall be done. He asked him to come back after a few days.

Meanwhile, Birbal called the merchant's friend and asked him, "Did you borrow one thousand Rupees from your merchant friend?" "No, sir. What proof does he have?" the friend asked. Without questioning him further, Birbal asked him to go.

The next day, Birbal summoned both the merchant and his friend. He gave a tin of ghee to each one of them and said, "Please sell this ghee for me." Taking the tins of ghee, they left. The merchant's friend didn't know that Birbal had dropped a gold coin in his tin to test his honesty.

After selling the ghee, the merchant and his friend went back to Birbal to give the money they had collected. Birbal asked the friend, "Did you get the gold coin from the tin?" Without any hesitation, he replied, "No, sir. I didn't."

Birbal quietly sent a soldier to his house to bring the son of merchant's friend. Birbal questioned the boy and found him to be very innocent and truthful. He disclosed it that his father had taken a gold coin out of the tin. When the son saw his father standing with the merchant, he said, "Father, have you returned the money that you had borrowed from uncle?"

Now, the father couldn't hide the truth. His face fell in shame. He asked Birbal for forgiveness. Birbal ordered the boy's father to return the merchant's money. He rewarded his son for his honesty and truthfulness. All the people present there praised Birbal for his wit and right justice.

AKBAR'S MARRIAGE

One day, the Queen asked King Akbar to remove Birbal and appoint her brother as Wazir. The King didn't like the idea. But then, he agreed to do so. The Queen said to the King, "Ask Birbal to make me apologise before you. If I don't do so you must dismiss him."

The next day, the King called Birbal and said, "You must make the queen apologize to me, otherwise I'll dismiss you from the office of Wazir."

Quietly, Birbal went out of the palace. He thought of a plan. He called a guard and whispered something into his ears. Then, he went to the palace to meet the Queen.

He started talking to the Queen without letting her know that he knew anything about the quarrel between her and the King. While he was busy talking to her, the guard entered into the room and said to Birbal, "Sir, the King is saying that everything has happened as per the plan."

As the queen heard this conversation, she asked Birbal, "Which plan is the guard talking about?" "Your Highness! I am not allowed to disclose it to anyone" replied Birbal. Now, the queen became very anxious and upset. She thought that the King might be planning to marry someone else because she had quarreled with him on the night before.

At once, she rushed to the King. With tears in her eyes, she apologized to him, "Please forgive me. I won't quarrel with you anymore. But, don't remarry." The king had a hearty laugh. He understood that Birbal, who was very intelligent, had succeeded in making the queen apologize to him. He praised Birbal for his cleverness.

THE OLD WOMAN'S MONEY-BAG

Once upon a time, an old woman decided to go on a pilgrimage. She went to her neighbour, named Vishnu and requested him to keep her bag full of money. But Vishnu refused to keep the bag and suggested that she bury it herself at a safer place.

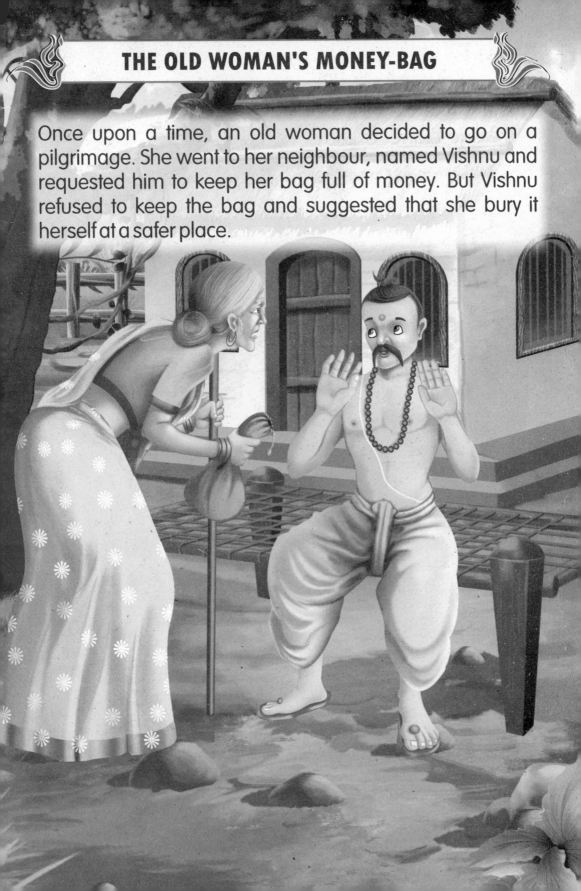

The old woman decided to bury the money bag near an old neem tree, at a small distance from her house. Vishnu who was a wicked man, secretly saw the place where the old woman had buried the money bag. When the woman left for pilgrimage, Vishnu went there at night and dug out the money bag. In its place, he buried another similar bag containing copper pieces.

After a few days, the old woman returned from pilgrimage. She went to the neem tree to dig out her money bag. She took it out. When she opened it, she was shocked to see copper pieces instead of gold coins in it. She started crying bitterly.

The old woman had heard a lot about Birbal's intelligence. So, she went to Birbal and told him the whole story. Birbal consoled her and promised to help her. He called Vishnu to the court and inquired about the missing money bag. However, Vishnu refused to know anything about the bag. He said, "Sir, I don't know anything about the bag."

Birbal called the village tailor. Upon seeing him, Vishnu's face turned pale. The tailor immediately recognized the bag and said, "This is the bag which Vishnu had brought to me for repair."

So, Vishnu was caught. He accepted his guilt. He apologized to Birbal and said, "Please forgive me for my wrong-doing." Birbal asked him to return the old woman's money bag containing the gold coins. Vishnu returned her money bag. She was happy. She praised Birbal for his wit and thanked him for his timely help.

THE TAILOR

Once Birbal told King Akbar that some workers were clever enough to steal some of the material they were given to work with. But Akbar didn't believe him.

In order to know the truth, the King called the royal tailor and asked him to stitch a blouse for his Queen. The tailor was asked to work in the palace under the vigil of guards.

After four days, the tailor's son called out his father from the window of the guarded room. He asked him, "Father, what have you been doing for the past four days?" The tailor trying to pacify his son, said, "Don't be upset. The blouse will be ready tonight."

The tailor somehow got an opportunity to play his game. He put the piece of cloth inside one of his shoes. He gave the shoe pair to his son.

The tailor stitched the blouse and it was given to the Queen. One day, the Queen saw a woman wearing a blouse made from the same cloth from which her blouse had been stitched. She complained about it to the King.

The tailor was called to the court and asked to speak the truth. He was told that if did not do so, he would be thrown out of the kingdom. The tailor asked for mercy and disclosed that when his son had come to meet him, he had put some of the cloth in his shoes and threw them at his son to express his anger. His son had taken it home. Later, his wife had stitched a blouse out of it.

Akbar accepted that Birbal was right. So, he praised Birbal for his alertness and wisdom.

THE OBSTINATE CHILD

Once King Akbar became very angry with Birbal since Birbal was late to the court. When he asked Birbal the reason for being so late, he said, "My Lord! My child had stopped me. He was not letting me come." But Akbar was not satisfied with his answer.

In order to convince Akbar, Birbal told him that he would act as a child and Akbar should try his best to satisfy his demands. Akbr allowed him to act as child.

So, Birbal began to threw tantrums like a spoiled child. He got on to Akbar's lap.

Akbar tried his best to make Birbal, the child, happy but all his efforts proved to be useless.

Crying bitterly, Birbal asked for a sugarcane. When the sugarcane was brought, he asked Akbar to chop it into small pieces. Although Akbar was irritated, he chopped the sugarcane into small pieces.

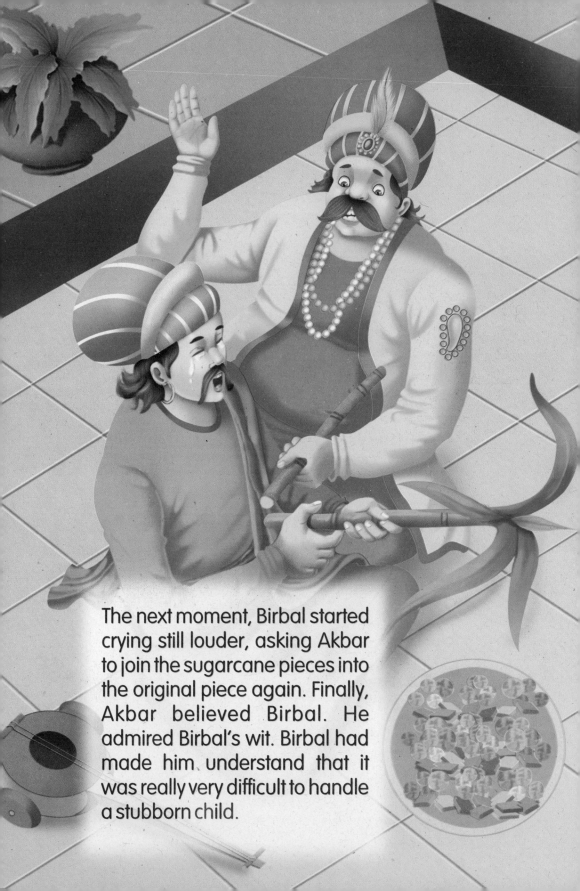

The next moment, Birbal started crying still louder, asking Akbar to join the sugarcane pieces into the original piece again. Finally, Akbar believed Birbal. He admired Birbal's wit. Birbal had made him understand that it was really very difficult to handle a stubborn child.

THE ANGRY MERCHANT

Once upon a time, there lived a very short-tempered man. His name was Krodhiram. One day, while eating food, he found a hair in his food.

He was very angry. He said to his wife, "Listen, this is your first mistake. So, I forgive you. But if ever, I find hair in my food again, I'll get your head shaved off."

After a few days, he again found a hair in his food. He became furious and sent for a barber to shave off his wife's head. His wife quietly sent a message to her four brothers for help. Then, she locked herself in a room.

Her brothers went to Birbal for help. Birbal said to them, "All of you go to your brother-in-law's house with shaven heads as if someone had died! I'll join you there soon."

The four brothers reached their sister's home with shaven heads. After some time, Birbal also came there with the arrangements for cremation.

Birbal ordered the boys to prepare the pyre for the last rites. The merchant was shocked to see all the preparations. Birbal told Krodhiram that he must die first because a woman's head could be shaved off only after she became a widow.

Now Krodhiram realized his mistake. He apologized to his wife, her brothers and Birbal for his misconduct. Everyone present there praised Birbal for his presence of mind and wisdom.

PANDITJI

Once upon a time, a man wished to became a Pandit. He had heard a lot about Birbal's wit and wisdom. So, he went to him and said, "Sir, I want to become a learned man. But I can't spend years in learning how to read or write. Please tell me a way out."

Birbal said, "Well, there is a way. Tomorrow, go and stand on any busy road. Some men will call you Panditji. If you want that everyone should address you as Panditji, run after them with a stick in your hand. But remember, show only your anger. Do not hit anyone."

The next day, he was walking down the road. Suddenly, some of Birbal's men started calling him, "Panditji! Panditji!" Soon, many children playing there joined them. They all started teasing him and said, "Panditji! Panditji!" The man lost his temper and ran after people with a stick in his hand.

Since that day, wherever he used to go, people on the way would make fun of him by calling him, "Panditji! Panditji!" Soon, the man was fed up of being called by this name by everyone.

Quite disturbed, he visited Birbal again and said, "Sir, I no longer wish to be addressed as Panditji. Now, everyone makes fun of me." Birbal advised him to leave the town and return after a gap of few years. In the course of time, people would forget him and his new name, Birbal told him.

The man followed Birbal's advice. He returned to the town after a long time. By that time, many people had forgotten him. No one made fun of him or called him Panditji. And even if anyone addressed him Panditji, he did not get irritated.
He admired Birbal for his intelligence. He also thanked him for making him realize that true happiness lies in being oneself.

TIT FOR TAT

Emperor Akbar was very fond of Birbal. He often used to play tricks with him. One day, he called a skilled carpenter and asked him to fix a magical device on the table in his room. He kept an apple on the table. He sent for Birbal to his room. He himself hid behind a curtain.

Birbal entered into the room and saw an apple lying on the table. He went near it to pick it up. As he touched it, his hand got stuck to the apple.

Immediately, the emperor came out and said mockingly, "Now, I understand that it is you who had been stealing small things from the palace. This time, I pardon you. Never do such an act again. You may go now." Birbal left the room, feeling badly insulted.

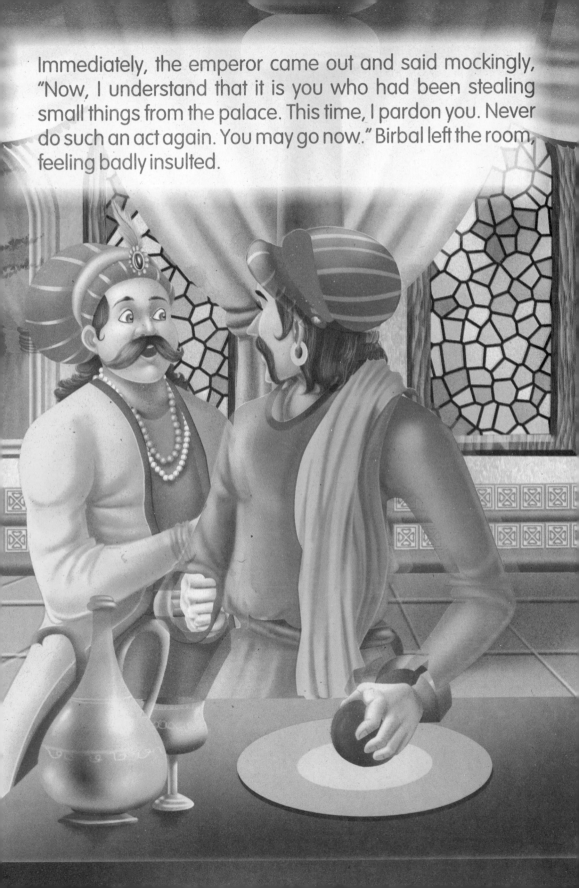

After a few days, Akbar went to a jungle for hunting. As he reached far deep in the jungle, he heard a loud cry, "Hey! Who are you? Just stop!"

The Emperor saw a big, ugly tribal man standing in front of him with a large bamboo stick. He shouted, "With whose permission have you entered this part of the jungle? I want to punish you. This time, I am permitting you to go. Before you leave, just say five times, "Like the God of Jungle." Akbar did so and returned to the palace, feeling quite ashamed.

The next day, when Birbal went to the palace, Akbar asked, "Birbal, how was the apple?" "Like the God of jungle," replied Birbal. The King was very pleased with the answer. He admired Birbal for his wit. Both of them smiled at each other and had laughed for a long time.

WHO IS MORE INTELLIGENT

One day, some courtiers, who were jealous of Birbal, went to Akbar and said, "Your Highness! Tansen is a renowned singer in the world. So why don't you appoint him as your Prime Minister instead of Birbal?" Akbar was not very pleased with the suggestion and said, "I'll see to it. But both of them have to undergo a test. And whosoever proves to be wiser, would become the Prime Minister."

The next day, Akbar called Birbal and Tansen and gave them a sealed letter each. He said, "Go and deliver this to the Emperor of Russia. You must return with its reply."

Birbal and Tansen reached Russia and handed over the letters to the Emperor of Russia. The Emperor opened the letter. It read : "Please hang these messengers." At once, the Emperor ordered his men to hang Birbal and Tansen.

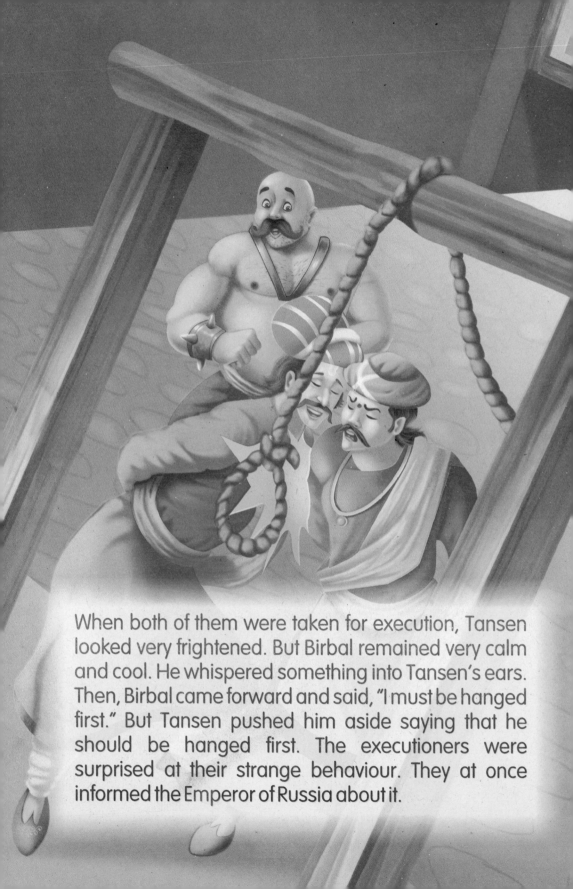

When both of them were taken for execution, Tansen looked very frightened. But Birbal remained very calm and cool. He whispered something into Tansen's ears. Then, Birbal came forward and said, "I must be hanged first." But Tansen pushed him aside saying that he should be hanged first. The executioners were surprised at their strange behaviour. They at once informed the Emperor of Russia about it.

The Emperor became very curious to know the reason for their strange behaviour. When asked, Birbal confided, "Sir, King Akbar's astrologer had suggested him that if you are made a sinner by killing his messengers, he can easily conquer you." The Empror of Russia changed his mind and ordered his men to set both of them free. He also gave them a letter that was to be given to King Akbar.

Birbal and Tansen came back to Akbar's court with the letter. Before Akbar could say anything, Tansen said to Akbar, "Your Highness! I don't deserve to be the Prime Minister. No one can beat Birbal in wit." All the other courtiers lowered their heads in shame.

THE THREE QUESTIONS

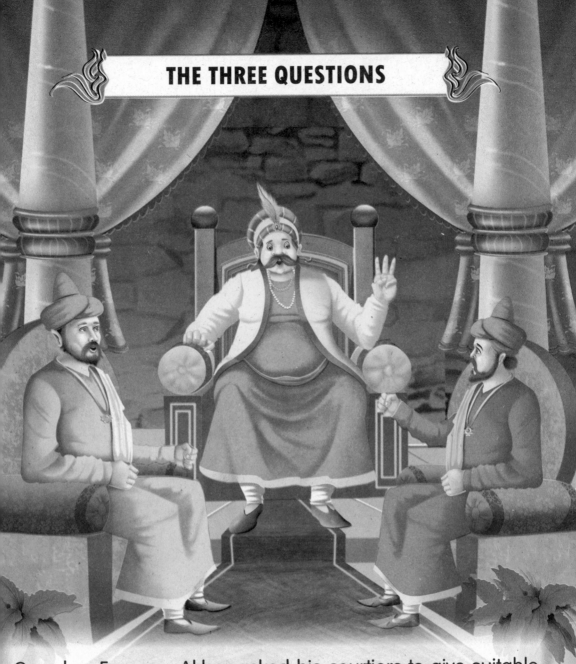

One day, Emperor Akbar asked his courtiers to give suitable answers to his three questions. Akbar asked, the following questions:

- What is it that exists today and shall remain so even tomorrow?
- What is it that exists today and shall not be there tomorrow?
- What is it that doesn't exist today but shall be there tomorrow?

All courtiers tried their best to answer these questions. But Akbar was not satisfied will their answers. When Birbal was asked, he said, "Your Majesty! In order to get suitable answers to your questions, you'll have to accompany me to the town in disguise."

Akbar and Birbal disguised themselves as saints and reached the market place. First, they went to a shop and asked the shopkeeper to donate one thousand Rupees to build a school. The shopkeeper gladly agreed. As they left the shop, Birbal said to Akbar, "Your highness! We have got the answer to your first question. Whatever the shopkeeper has today, shall remain with him. Also, his good intentions would help him earn in the future as well."

As they went ahead, they came across a beggar who was enjoying some food. He had got it as alms. Birbal asked him to share his food with them. He became angry and refused to share his food. Birbal turned to Akbar and said, "Your Majesty! Here is the answer to your second question. The selfishness of the beggar will not let him have in the future what he has got today."

Now, they walked further. At some distance, he saw a hermit meditating under a tree. Birbal offered him some money. But the hermit refused to take it and said, "I am not interested in worldly pleasures." Birbal said, "Your Majesty! You have got the answer to your third question. Today, this holy man has sacrificed the worldly pleasures but in his next birth, he would be able to enjoy them."

He further said, "You too have a good life as an Emperor because of your good deeds of the past. You'll have such a life in the future too, if you continue to be good and helpful to others."

The Emperor was satisfied with Birbal's answers and appreciated his wisdom.

BIRBAL'S KHICHDI

It was winter. All ponds were frozen. At the court, Akbar asked Birbal, "Tell me Birbal, will a man do anything for money?" Birbal replied, "Yes, your Majesty."
The Emperor ordered him to prove it. The next day, Birbal came to the court along with a poor Brahmin. His family was starving. Birbal told the King that the Brahmin was ready to do anything for the sake of money.

The King ordered the Brahmin to remain inside the frozen pond throughout the night without any clothes, if he needed money. The whole night, the poor Brahmin stood inside the pond, shivering with cold. He returned to the court the next day to receive the reward.

The King asked, "You first tell me, how could you withstand the extreme cold, throughout the night?" The innocent Brahmin replied, "I could see the lamp that was lit in the palace." Akbar refused to pay him his reward, saying, "You got warmth from the lamp and it saved you from the cold. So, you'll not get your reward." The poor Brahmin could not argue with him and went back home, totally disappointed.

Birbal tried to explain to the King but he was in no mood to listen to Birbal . Birbal was very displeased with the King and did not go to the court.

When Birbal didn't turn up even on the next day, Akbar himself went to Birbal's house. Akbar saw that Birbal had lit a fire. At a height of one yard from the fire, he had kept a pot of uncooked khichdi. The King questioned him, "How will this khichdi get cooked with the fire that is one yard away? What is wrong with you Birbal?"

Birbal replied, "My Lord! When it is possible for a person to receive warmth from a lamp that is one mile away, it is possible to cook the khichdi which is just one yard away from the fire."

Akbar smiled. He had understood his mistake. He admired Birbal for his intelligence and correct reasoning. He called the poor Brahmin and rewarded him with gold coins. The poor Brahmin was very happy.

THE TURBAN COMPETITION

King Akbar praised Birbal's way of tying his turban in his court at one point of time. Upon hearing Birbal's praise, a chief, named Mullah-do-Pyaza, felt very jealous and said, "What is so great about it? I can tie the turban in a much better way than Birbal."

King Akbar asked Mullah to prove his ability the next day. Mullah was very thrilled.

The next day, he reached the court quite early. All courtiers praised him for tying the turban; it was really better than Birbal. Akbar came along with Birbal and was very pleased. He praised Mullah and said, "Really this turban has been tied in a much better way than Birbal."

Birbal said, "Your Majesty! Mullah has not tied the turban himself. His wife has tied it for him. Let Mullah untie his turban and tie it again in this court. Then only, should you decide who can tie the turban in a better way."

The King agreed with Birbal. So, he asked Mullah to take off his turban and tie it again in front of everyone. Mullah took off his turban. But he couldn't tie it again without the help of a mirror.

Birbal smiled and asked him, "What is the problem, Mullah?" Mullah didn't say anything and tried his best to tie the turban. In the absence of the mirror, he tied the turban in such an untidy manner that all people in the court started laughing at him.

King Akbar said, "So, Birbal was right, Mullah! It is not you but your wife who is worthy of all the praise." Mullah had nothing to say and felt extremely ashamed.

However, all courtiers and the King showered praise on Birbal due to his wit and wisdom.

BIRBAL'S JUSTICE

Once a middle-aged woman came to Akbar's court. That woman was dragging a man along with her. She came before Akbar and complained, "O My Lord! This man has snatched all my jewelry." Akbar asked Birbal to solve the case.

Birbal called both of them. First of all, he asked the man, "Have you snatched this woman's jewelry?" The man folded both his hands and replied, "No, sir! She is lying. I have not taken her jewelry."

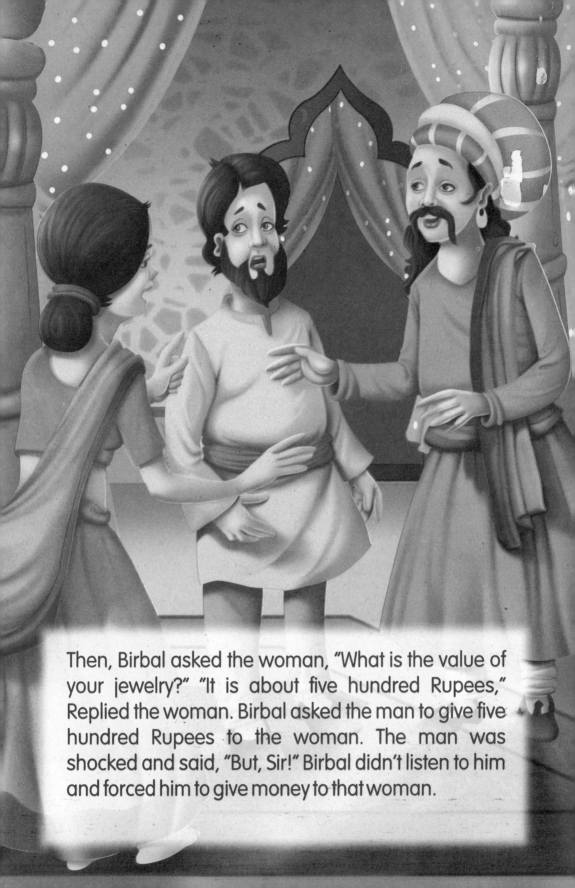

Then, Birbal asked the woman, "What is the value of your jewelry?" "It is about five hundred Rupees," Replied the woman. Birbal asked the man to give five hundred Rupees to the woman. The man was shocked and said, "But, Sir!" Birbal didn't listen to him and forced him to give money to that woman.

The woman was happy to get money and went away.

As she left, Birbal called the man and asked him to run after the woman and snatch five hundred Rupees from her. The man was really confused. But he ran fast to chase the woman.

After a while, the woman came back crying and said, "Sir, this man was now trying to rob me of my money." Birbal asked her, "Did he really take the money?" "No, Sir. He tried his best but I didn't allow him. You must punish him, my Lord," said the woman.

To everyone's surprise, Birbal announced, "Punishment will be given but to you—the clever woman. This man is innocent. This man, who couldn't snatch even five hundred Rupees, can never snatch jewelry from you."

The wicked woman requested Birbal to pardon her. Birbal took mercy on her. He asked the woman to return five hundred Rupees to the man. The man thanked Birbal for the justice.

King Akbar called Birbal and praised him for his wit in solving the case tactfully.

AKBAR'S MOUSTACHE

One day, the Emperor was relaxing in his chamber.

The queen brought their son and put him in his lap.
King Akbar took him in his arms and started playing
with him.

While playing, the little prince caught hold of Akbar's moustache and twisted it hard. With much difficulty, he freed himself from the boy's grip.

The next day, when Akbar came to the court he asked the courtiers, "What punishment should be given if someone pulls your moustache?" Everybody gave different suggestions but nobody's reply satisfied the Emperor.

Of all the courtiers, Akbar trusted Birbal the most and admired him for his wisdom. So, he asked Birbal to answer his question.

Birbal replied, "Your Majesty! He should be offered sweets." The Emperor smiled at this reply and asked, "Why should he be offered sweets?"

Birbal said, "Your Highness! The person twisting your moustache can be none other than your own child." Akbar was very pleased with the answer and praised Birbal for his wit and wisdom.